Teachers, librarians, and kids from across Canada are talking about the *Canadian Flyer Adventures.* Here's what some of them had to say:

I love the fact that these are Canadian adventures—kids should know how exciting Canadian history is. Emily and Matt are regular kids, full of curiosity, and I can see readers relating to them. ~ *JEAN K., TEACHER, ONTARIO*

What kids told us:

I would like to have the chance to ride on a magical sled and have adventures. ~ *EMMANUEL*

I would like to tell the author that her book is amazing, incredible, awesome, and a million times better than any book I've read. ~ *MARIA*

I would recommend the *Canadian Flyer Adventures* series to other kids so they could learn about Canada too. The book is just the right length and hard to put down. ~ *PAUL*

The books I usually read are the full-of-fact encyclopedias. This book is full of interesting ideas that simply grab me. ~ *ELEANOR*

At the end of the book Matt and Emily say they are going on another adventure. I'm very interested in where they are going next! ~ *ALEX*

I like when Emily and Matt fly into the sky on a sled towards a new adventure. I can't wait for the next book! ~ *JI SANG*

On the Case

Frieda Wishinsky

Illustrated by Jean-Paul Eid

MAPLE
TREE
PRESS

For my friend and fellow author Eve Feldman

Many thanks to the hard-working Maple Tree/Owlkids team, for their insightful comments and steadfast support. Special thanks to Jean-Paul Eid and Barb Kelly for their engaging and energetic illustrations and design.

Maple Tree Press books are published by Owlkids Books Inc.
10 Lower Spadina Avenue, Suite 400, Toronto, Ontario M5V 2Z2
www.owlkids.com

Distributed in Canada by Raincoast Books
9050 Shaughnessy Street, Vancouver, British Columbia V6P 6E5

Distributed in the United States by Publishers Group West
1700 Fourth Street, Berkeley, California 94710

Library and Archives Canada Cataloguing in Publication

Wishinsky, Frieda
On the case / Frieda Wishinsky ; illustrated by Jean-Paul Eid.

(Canadian flyer adventures ; 12)
ISBN 978-1-897349-54-0 (bound).--ISBN 978-1-897349-55-7 (pbk.)

1. Steele, Samuel B. (Samuel Benfield), 1848-1919--Juvenile
fiction. 2. North West Mounted Police (Canada)--Juvenile
fiction. I. Eid, Jean-Paul II. Title.
III. Series: Wishinsky, Frieda . Canadian flyer adventures ; 12.
PS8595.I834O5 2009   jC813'.54   C2009-901009-7

Library of Congress Control Number: 2009923333

  Conseil des Arts   Canada Council    ONTARIO ARTS COUNCIL
                       du Canada   for the Arts   CONSEIL DES ARTS DE L'ONTARIO

We acknowledge the financial support of the Canada Council for the Arts, the Ontario Arts Council, the Government of Canada through the Book Publishing Industry Development Program (BPIDP), and the Government of Ontario through the Ontario Media Development Corporation's Book Initiative for our publishing activities.

Printed in Canada
Ancient Forest Friendly: Printed on 100% Post-Consumer Recycled Paper

A   B   C   D   E   F

CONTENTS

HOW IT ALL BEGAN

Emily and Matt couldn't believe their luck. They discovered an old dresser full of strange objects in the tower of Emily's house. They also found a note from Emily's Great-Aunt Miranda: "The sled is yours. Fly it to wonderful adventures."

They found a sled right behind the dresser! When they sat on it, shimmery gold words appeared:

Rub the leaf
Three times fast.
Soon you'll fly
To the past.

The sled rose over Emily's house. It flew over their town of Glenwood. It sailed out of a cloud and into the past. Their adventures on the flying sled had begun! Where will the sled take them next? Turn the page to find out.

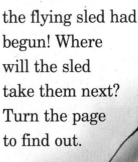

Fort Steele,
1888

1

Mountie Sam

"You have to watch this movie. It's my favourite," said Matt's Grandma Sophie.

Emily and Matt curled up on her couch. Grandma Sophie sat beside them. Her green eyes sparkled. "It's so romantic!" she said.

"Romantic," groaned Matt.

Grandma Sophie laughed. "It's full of adventure, too."

"That sounds better," said Matt.

"What's it called?" asked Emily.

"*Rose Marie.*"

"Is it only about girls?" asked Matt.

"No. There's also an officer from the North-West Mounted Police."

"I love Mounties!" said Emily, winking at Matt. "Don't you, Matt?"

Matt nodded. They'd met one Mountie, Sam Steele, on their Yukon adventure during the Gold Rush.

"Mounties are cool," said Matt. "But what's this one doing with a girl called Rose Marie?"

"Her brother's been accused of murder. The officer is bringing the brother to justice. But that's all I'll tell you. I don't want to spoil the movie. You'll love it. It's full of beautiful scenery, amazing horseback riding, and singing."

"A singing Mountie?" Matt made a face.

"He doesn't sing all the time," said Grandma Sophie. "Just once in a while. Here." Grandma Sophie passed them a bowl. "I made popcorn."

"Great," said Emily, laughing. "Movies about singing Mounties are much better with popcorn."

"It still sounds way too romantic to me," said Matt.

"Just watch," said Grandma Sophie. "Let's start the show!"

Grandma Sophie clicked on the movie. Matt flipped off the lights in the den.

"It's in black and white!" said Emily as the movie began. "I've never seen a whole movie in black and white. It's weird without colour."

"Look! There's the Mountie," said Matt.

"And there's Rose Marie," said Emily. "Pass the popcorn, please."

Emily and Matt could tell that Grandma Sophie knew all the scenes and songs. She kept pointing to the screen and saying, "The next scene is terrific," or, "Wait till you hear this song."

Emily and Matt weren't used to movies where people sang as if they were in an opera. When everybody sang, the children felt like laughing. They bit their lips so they wouldn't. They didn't want Grandma Sophie to think they were making fun of her favourite movie.

In the last scene, the main actors gazed into each other's eyes and sang a love song.

"I know it's an old-fashioned movie," said Grandma Sophie as the words "The End" flashed across the screen. "But I still love it."

"It was fun," said Emily, "even if some of it was romantic."

"The adventure parts were good," said Matt. "I wish I could ride a horse in the Rocky Mountains and investigate a murder with a Mountie."

"Hmmm," said Emily, winking at Matt. "Maybe you can."

2

Button Up

"Were you thinking what I was thinking?" asked Emily, walking back from Grandma Sophie's house.

"That *Rose Marie* was a goofy movie?"

"Yes, but also that it would be great to see Sam Steele again. During the movie, every time I saw the Mountie, I remembered how we met Sam Steele during the Gold Rush."

"Imagine if Sam Steele sang as he saved all those people from drowning in the Yukon River," said Matt, laughing.

"Like this: Hurry, everybody! Get out of that sinking boat!" sang Emily in a deep voice.

"Yes, singing in the middle of danger is weird. But it would be awesome to watch Sam Steele investigate a real murder! I bet he did. Mounties were the same as police officers."

"Come on! Let's check the tower room. Maybe there's something there that will fly us to meet him again."

Emily and Matt raced to Emily's house. They zoomed up the rickety stairs to the tower room.

Emily stood in front of the dresser that held all the magic objects. "Which drawer should we check first: one, two, three, or four?"

"Let's try drawer number three," said Matt.

Emily slid the drawer open. She peered inside.

"Well?" said Matt.

"You're a genius," said Emily.

"Why?"

"Look what's here." Emily pulled out a tarnished brass button with a label.

Matt read the label out loud. "Fort Steele, 1888. Awesome! I bet we'll find Sam Steele in a fort named after him."

"Well, he might be there. The label says 1888. That's before the Gold Rush, so he probably won't be in the Yukon. Where is Fort Steele, anyway?"

"Maybe it's somewhere out West," said Matt. "I wonder if Sam Steele will remember us?"

"How could he? If we meet Sam Steele in 1888, he'll be ten years younger than he was the first time we met him!" Emily laughed. "Time travel makes things pretty complicated."

Matt grinned. "Thinking about spinning through time makes my head spin. But it's fun, even if we never really know what will happen till it happens. Let's go to Fort Steele and see if Sam Steele is there!"

"I have my sketchbook. Do you have your digital recorder?" asked Emily.

Matt patted his pocket. "It's here, like always."

Emily pulled the Canadian Flyer out from behind the dresser. She hopped on the sled, and Matt followed. As soon as they were seated, shimmery gold words appeared.

Rub the leaf
Three times fast.
Soon you'll fly
To the past.

Emily rubbed the maple leaf. Immediately the sled was enveloped in thick fog. When the fog lifted, they rose over Emily's house, over Glenwood, and toward a fluffy white cloud.

"We're on our way!" sang Emily in her deep opera voice.

"You're not going to sing all the way through this adventure, are you?" asked Matt as they headed into the cloud.

"Maybe or maybe not!" sang Emily in a high-pitched voice.

"Oh no," groaned Matt.

3

Here Comes Sam!

When the sled burst out of the cloud, it dipped towards the ground.

"We're going down," said Matt. "But I don't see a fort. Do you?"

Emily pointed to some log buildings to their right. "That looks like a fort. It's almost like the ones I used to build with my log set. But the one down there looks even more crooked than mine."

"We're not going to the fort. We're heading towards a town!" said Matt as the sled suddenly turned.

"Hold on," said Emily. "We're going lower. We're about to land."

The sled bumped down on dusty ground. There were loose pebbles everywhere. Matt and Emily slid off the sled.

"This looks like cowboy country," said Matt, peering around. "It's dry and dusty like in those old cowboy movies. See all those hitching posts for horses?" Then Matt looked at his clothes. "Did the magic make me look like a cowboy?"

He wore a pair of blue pants, a light brown shirt, and ankle-high boots.

"A little," said Emily. "What about me?"

Emily wore a white blouse, a skirt past her knees, and ankle-high brown boots.

"You look kind of like a cowgirl. If we had cool cowboy hats, we'd really look ready for the Old West," said Matt.

"I wish I had a cool hat to keep the sun out

of my eyes. It's so hot and sunny around here," said Emily, squinting to see the mountains in the distance.

Matt pointed to a small general store. "Check out the sign on that store. It says Galbraith's Ferry General Store. Weren't we supposed to land in Fort Steele?"

"Don't worry. The sled always takes us to the right place," said Emily.

"Well, up till now it has, but I don't see anyone around. Maybe we're in one of those ghost towns."

"I see someone!" said Emily, pointing. "He's over there, riding towards that low wooden building! Look! Do you think it could be—?"

"Yes! He's wearing a Mountie uniform, and there are shiny buttons on his jacket. He's tall. It might be Sam Steele. Let's get closer and find out."

Matt and Emily raced towards the rider.

"Excuse us, sir," Matt called, but the rider and his horse were too far away to hear.

"Sir! Sir!" called Emily, waving as she chased after them.

By the time the rider slowed to approach the building, Emily had caught up with them. She was so close she could almost touch the horse's tail.

As the rider turned to see who was calling him, Emily yelled, "Hello, sir!" so loudly that she startled the horse. It neighed. Then it kicked.

Emily jumped out of the way before the horse could kick her in the teeth. She slipped on some loose gravel and fell on her rear.

"Are you all right, young lady?" asked the Mountie.

"I think so," said Emily. She dusted herself off and struggled to her feet.

"What do you think you were doing?" asked the Mountie. "You never approach a horse from the rear. Don't you know anything about horses?"

"Not much. You see, we...we..." muttered Emily. She didn't know how to explain that they were here to meet Sam Steele. And yes. She was sure now! He was Sam Steele! Of course, he was younger than during the Gold Rush. But he was as tall as she remembered. His voice was strong and firm, just like it had been when he ordered all the people in rickety boats off the raging Yukon River.

"Are you Sam Steele?" Matt blurted out.

"I am. And who are you, and what are you doing in Galbraith's Ferry?"

4

Who Did It?

"I'm Emily and...we're visiting."

"And I'm Matt. We're so glad to meet you, Superintendent Steele."

"How do you know who I am?" asked Sam Steele. "I don't think I've met you two before."

"You're famous," said Emily.

Sam Steele threw his head back and laughed. "I'm not famous. I'm just a Superintendent of the North-West Mounted Police doing his job. And my job now is to hurry inside that building and proceed with a murder investigation."

"Murder!" said Matt.

"Investigation!" said Emily.

"That's correct. There's been a lot of unrest around here lately. As a matter of fact, you two shouldn't be wandering around. I wouldn't want to see you get hurt," replied Sam Steele.

"We'll be careful," said Emily.

"Can we go inside and hear what happens at the investigation? We've never seen a murder investigation except—" Matt was about to say, except on TV or in the movies. But he caught himself. Sam Steele would have no idea what he was talking about.

"No," said Steele. "I do not allow children into my investigations. Why don't you head back to wherever you're visiting? Where did you say that was?"

"We were supposed to visit Fort Steele, the place named after you," said Emily.

Sam Steele howled with laughter. "Where do you two get your strange ideas? Imagine, a place named after me. Why would anyone do that?"

"I don't know," said Emily, "but they did. Well, at least that's what we heard."

"Well you heard wrong. Now, off this street. And as for you, young lady, no more scaring horses or one day you're really going to lose your teeth!"

Sam Steele tied his horse to a post and strode into the building.

"What now?" asked Emily. "He wants us to get out of here, but there's no one around to bother us."

"And we've come all this way. We have to see what's going on in that investigation."

"We can't do that. You heard Mr. Steele. No kids allowed."

"No kids allowed inside the building, but we can watch from somewhere else," said Matt.

"Like where?"

"Like over there." Matt pointed to a window at the side of the building. "Let's grab those crates and stand on them. Maybe we can see into the investigation room and hear what's happening."

Emily patted Matt on the back. "That's a brilliant idea, cowboy," she said.

The friends grabbed the sled and headed for the back of the building. As they were putting down their sled, they saw two dark-haired young boys run towards the building where the investigation was being held. Five older boys wearing overalls were chasing after them.

"Get those Indians!" shouted the tallest boy.

5

Taking Sides

"Liars!"

"Thieves!"

"Murderers!"

The five older boys had surrounded the First Nations boys and were shouting at them.

"Hey! What are you doing?" yelled Emily, running up to them.

"Leave them alone!" hollered Matt as he caught up to her.

"Whose side are you on, anyway?" snarled the tall boy.

"We're on nobody's side," said Matt.

"You heard Judd. You have to take sides," growled his friend.

"And if you don't, get out of here," said Judd.

The frightened First Nations boys tried to break through the circle the bigger boys had made around them. But they couldn't. The settler boys were bigger, and there were more of them.

"Let them out," said Emily, tugging at Judd's shirt.

"What do you think you're doing?" snapped Judd. "Get your hands off my shirt, you stupid girl."

"Don't call me stupid," said Emily, but she took her hands off Judd's shirt. She didn't want to rip it. Who knew what he'd do then?

"These Indians," said Judd, pointing to

the boys, "are liars, cheats, and stupid, just like their cousins inside that courthouse. And anyone who takes their side is just like them. That Mountie better make sure that the men inside hang."

"Sam Steele is going to be fair. If the accused men are innocent, he'll let them go," said Matt.

"What do you know?" said Judd. "Who are you, anyway? Get out of here."

"We're not going anywhere," said Matt.

"We're not leaving till you let those boys go," said Emily.

"Oh yeah?" snapped Judd. Then Judd let go of his friend's hand, turned to Emily, and yanked her ponytail, hard.

"Ouch!" she yelped. She was about to kick Judd in the shins, when a girl of about eleven ran out of the general store.

"Stop, Judd!" the girl cried, "or I'm going to tell Pa. He'll be angry."

"Pa's away, and this is none of your business, Sarah," said Judd.

"Only cowards hurt girls," said Sarah, standing beside Emily.

Emily's head was still smarting from the hard yank on her hair, but she smiled at Sarah. "Thanks," she said.

"I apologize for my brother's rude behaviour," said Sarah. "Ma's home with our new baby brother, and Pa's been away working on the railroad. He'd never allow Judd to behave like this."

Then she turned to her brother and his friends who were still encircling the terrified First Nations boys.

"Let them go," she said.

"I told you before, Sarah," Judd growled. "This is none of your business. Take your stupid friends and get out of here."

"We'll take care of these Indians in our own way," said Judd. Then he and his friends tightened the circle around the boys.

"We have to do something to stop them," whispered Matt.

"I don't know how to stop them," said Sarah. "My brother and his friends are strong and tough. And Pa won't be back till tomorrow."

6

Enough!

"We have to get someone to help before those two kids are hurt," said Matt quietly.

"Let's ask Sam Steele to help," Emily whispered. "I don't think the investigation has started. I bet Judd and his friends will run if they see Superintendent Steele."

"My brother is stubborn," said Sarah. "But you're right. We have to do something. I don't want anything terrible to happen. Those children didn't do anything."

Emily, Matt, and Sarah ran into the

building Sam Steele had entered. They saw Superintendent Steele speaking to a group of men. There was no sign of the prisoners yet.

Matt cleared his throat. "Excuse me, Superintendent Steele," he said.

Sam Steele spun around. He pursed his lips and gave Matt a disapproving look. "What are you doing here?"

"We're sorry, but we really need your help outside," said Emily.

"And we need it now," said Sarah. "Something bad might happen if you don't come."

"What's this all about?" asked Steele.

"My brother Judd and his friends are about to beat up two little Indian kids," said Sarah. "And Judd won't listen to us."

Sam Steele peered out the door behind them.

Judd and his friends were still circling the two First Nations boys and screaming insults at them. The two little boys looked frightened, but they didn't move or say anything.

Then the circle around them grew tighter and the insults became more threatening. The bigger boys began to kick gravel at the First Nations boys.

Without a word, Sam Steele marched out the door.

Emily, Matt, and Sarah stepped aside to let

him pass, then raced after him.

"My name is Superintendent Sam Steele," he barked at the bigger boys, "and I am with the North-West Mounted Police. I order you to leave those boys alone."

7

Go Home

"A Mountie!" yelped Judd. He dropped his friends' hands and spun around. Sam Steele glared at him.

"I...I...I'm sorry, sir. It's just that these Indians are...are...no good," Judd stammered.

The two First Nations boys stared at Sam Steele towering angrily over their tormentors.

"Go home now, all of you. And if I ever hear that you've been menacing these children again, you'll answer to me," said Sam Steele.

Judd glared at Emily and Matt for a

moment. "I won't bother anyone, sir," he said.

"What do you have to say for yourselves?" Sam Steele stared at Judd's friends.

"We won't do anything either, sir," they muttered.

"I'm going to be around these parts for a long time, and if I hear that any of you has caused mischief, I guarantee you'll regret it. Understood, gentlemen?"

"Understood," said all the boys.

Then they turned on their heels and ran off like scared rabbits.

"You were right to call me," said Steele to Emily, Matt, and Sarah.

The friends smiled.

"And are you boys all right?" Steele asked the two little First Nations children.

They nodded but said nothing. Then the younger of the two boys ran over, threw

his arms around the
Mountie, and hugged
him.

Sam Steele swallowed
and cleared his throat.
"Go back to your homes,
children," he murmured.
Emily and Matt knew he
was glad that he'd helped
the two boys.

"Now, it's time I
returned to my duties.
I have a murder to
investigate," said Steele.
He walked back inside.

The two little boys
smiled at Matt, Emily,
and Sarah. Then they
ran off.

"Now what?" asked Emily.

"We came to see a murder investigation, and that's what we're going to do! I still want to hear what's going on," said Matt. "Let's stand on those crates like we planned. We'll keep our word to Sam Steele. We won't take a step inside the building."

"Sounds good to me!" said Emily. "Do you want to come too, Sarah?"

"I have to go home and help my mother with the baby. But I'm glad I wasn't alone to deal with Judd. He's only a year older than me, but sometimes he acts like a brat. He loves showing off for his friends."

Emily and Matt waved to Sarah as she dashed off.

"Let's move the sled and get those crates," said Matt.

"The sled?" said Emily, peering around.

"Where is it, Matt?"

Matt and Emily looked up and down the dusty streets for the sled.

"Oh no! Someone must have taken it," said Emily.

"And you know who probably did," said Matt.

"It had to be them. How do we find them, and how do we get it back?"

"I don't know, but we'd better find them soon. Who knows what they'll do to the sled after we called Sam Steele out on them? And if anything happens to the sled..." Matt gulped, "we may never get back home."

8

Don't Sit On It!

"Is this what you're looking for?" Judd strutted out from behind a building with his friends. He was pulling the sled.

"Yes. Now can you please give it back?" said Emily.

"Are you joking? We found it. It's ours."

"You didn't find it. You took it," said Matt.

"So what? If you cared so much about your sled, you wouldn't have left it laying around like it was garbage," said Judd.

Emily and Matt glanced at each other.

Emily knew that Matt was thinking they had to move quickly and get the sled back from those boys. Judd and his friends were angry that Matt and Emily had called Sam Steele to rescue the First Nations boys. They wanted revenge. What if their revenge was to destroy the sled?

"We're going to have a nice little ride on this sled," said Judd. "I'm going to get Rusty, my pa's horse, and then we'll hitch the sled to him and take turns having a ride."

"Too bad Rusty is such an unpredictable horse. He sometimes takes off like a crazy animal," said one of his friends.

"Yes. You never know what Rusty might do," said Judd. He shook his head and smirked at Emily and Matt.

Then he turned to his friends. "Stand guard over the sled while I get Rusty. He's hitched

around the corner."

Two of Judd's friends held the sled's rope. They glared at Emily and Matt.

Emily and Matt didn't know what to do. How could they get their sled back? They couldn't bother Sam Steele again. This wasn't a fight. He wouldn't want to be interrupted over a sled.

Soon Judd was back leading a reddish-brown horse. Emily and Matt could see that Rusty was a jumpy animal. He neighed and pranced around. It was hard for Judd to keep him standing in one place. Rusty looked as if he could take off in any direction. If the sled was attached to that wild horse, he might gallop off and break it in no time.

Emily gulped. Matt wiped sweat off his face. They had to come up with something, anything, fast.

"You might not want to sit on that sled," Emily blurted out.

"Why not?" said Judd. "It looks comfortable to me."

"Because...because...of that!" exclaimed Emily. As she spoke, a skunk emerged from behind one of the crates. The boys shrieked and Rusty neighed as the skunk lifted its tail and sprayed the sled!

9

Stinky!

"Take your stinky sled! I don't want to touch it!" screeched Judd, making a face.

Matt held his nose and ran over. "Yuck," he muttered as he picked the rope up and pulled the sled over towards Emily.

"Come on," said Judd. "Let's get out of here. They'll never get the stink off that sled."

Judd pulled on Rusty's lead.

Rusty neighed and reared and Judd's leg got caught in the rope. Judd's friends raced over to help him untangle himself.

"Hurry!" said Emily. "The sled smells awful but we have to take it." She swallowed hard, trying not to barf as they ran towards the back of the building where the murder investigation was about to take place.

Halfway there, Emily and Matt glanced back. They saw Judd's friends untangle him from Rusty, but Rusty still pranced around as if he'd been bitten in the rear by a bee.

"That was too close for comfort," said Matt. "Come on. Let's hide the sled so we can climb up on the crates and watch. Otherwise, while we're busy looking, someone might take it again."

"The sooner we hide it, the better," said Emily. "If I smell the sled for another minute, I'll be sick. Look. There's a shack behind the building. Let's see what's inside it. Maybe we can hide the sled in there."

Emily and Matt opened the door to the shack. It looked like no one had been inside for a while. There was only a broken chair, a rickety table, and a pile of blankets in one corner.

"Should we hide the sled under those blankets?" said Emily.

Matt shoved the sled under the pile of blankets. Then they walked back to the main building. "Look! I think they're bringing the prisoners into the building. I bet the investigation will start now."

Matt climbed up onto a crate and peeked through the dirty window.

"It's hard to see. The window is smeared," he told Emily. "I wish we had something to clean it with, but I don't even have a handkerchief."

Emily started to climb up too, but the window wasn't big enough for both of them.

"I can hardly hear anything, but I can see the room filling up with people," said Matt.

"Open the window a little so I can hear something," said Emily.

Matt tried to open the window, but it was stuck. "It's so dirty and sticky, it won't budge," he said.

"Come on. Try again," said Emily.

Matt yanked at the bottom of the window. Nothing. He jiggled it over and over. It finally began to open.

"Hooray!" sang Emily. "You did it."

"Shh. I don't want them to know we're here, Em. Sam Steele just called the investigation to order."

10

Oops!

Matt leaned over the small window. "It's still hard to hear," he whispered to Emily. "I'm going to lean over a bit more."

"Be careful," said Emily in a low voice. "You don't want to fall in."

"Don't worry. I won't."

Matt started to hoist himself up onto the ledge. He leaned in over the edge of the window. Good! He could hear much better now.

"What are they saying?" Emily whispered.

"Wow! You won't believe this!" said Matt.

He turned to tell Emily that the prisoners had just proclaimed their innocence. But as he did, he lost his balance and slipped. He fell forward, through the open window and into the room!

"Help!" screamed Matt.

"Matt!" screamed Emily.

Emily scrambled up the crate and looked in the open window. The people in the room were gathered around Matt, blocking her view. Everyone was talking and yelling at once.

"The boy is hurt."

"Can he move?"

"Is he dead?"

Dead?

Emily's mouth went dry. She had to find out what happened to Matt. She couldn't stay on this crate.

She hopped off the crates and raced to the front of the building. She charged inside just in time to see Matt sit up.

Phew! He was alive! He was moving.

He'd landed on a pile of blankets. The blankets had saved his life!

Someone was bringing him a drink of water. He looked a little dazed, but he was sipping the water. Emily ran over to the crowd surrounding him.

"Please, let me speak to Matt. He's my friend," she said.

"Let her through," said Sam Steele.

The people around Matt made a pathway. Emily ran over to Matt. "I thought you were dead," she said. Tears rolled down her cheeks. She wiped them away with her sleeve.

"Are you crying?" said Matt. "You must have really been worried."

"Of course I was worried, silly," said Emily. "You could have broken your neck."

"Your friend is right. That was foolish, young man," said Steele. "It's lucky Chief Isadore and his people brought blankets with them to trade. Now that we know you're in one piece, we can continue the investigation. I hope we'll have no further interruptions."

Matt stood up. He tried to take a step, but his legs were wobbly.

"You're in no condition to walk. Sit down here," said Steele. "But not one more word out of either of you till this investigation is completed."

"We promise," said Emily, helping Matt to a bench in the back of the room.

"Now, let us continue," said Steele. "We have heard from the prisoners. Is there anyone who has any evidence against these two men?"

11

Order in the Court

Emily nudged Matt as the investigation continued. She mouthed the word innocent to him. Matt nodded. There was no evidence that the two First Nations men, Kapula and Little Isadore, had committed the murder.

Emily smiled. It was hard not to talk to Matt while the investigation was going on, but they'd promised they'd be quiet, and they were going to keep their word. They'd already disrupted everything!

But the men in front of them were not quiet.

"Those two Indians are going to get off!" grumbled one of the men. He had a long, scruffy black beard.

"That Mountie likes Indians more than white people," said his friend, who was noisily chewing tobacco.

A short man in front of them turned around. "Steele is fair and just," he said. "He's going by the evidence. Let him finish this investigation. And if the men are innocent, we have to honour that verdict."

"I don't have to honour anything," boomed the bearded man.

"Order in the court!" said Sam Steele. He banged the table with his fist. He glared at the man who'd interrupted him.

The man grimaced and poked his friend in the ribs. "Indian lovers," he muttered.

Emily didn't know if Steele heard what the

bearded man said. If he did, he ignored it.

The investigation continued.

"Kapula and Little Isadore," said Steele finally. He looked directly at the two accused men. "Please stand."

The two First Nations men stood. They placed their hands at their sides and waited for Steele's verdict.

"I have heard all the evidence and listened to all the witnesses. I am now certain that there is no evidence you were involved with this murder. Neither of you was near the place where the men were killed. I therefore proclaim you both innocent of the charges. You are free to go."

A cheer rose from Chief Isadore and his men. Little Isadore and Kapula hugged each other. A few settlers applauded, but others grumbled.

"They're guilty as sin. I don't care what Steele says. He's an outsider. What does he know, anyway?" said the bearded man.

"This is not justice! This is—nothing." His friend spit his tobacco out on the floor, as if to show what he thought of the investigation and Sam Steele.

Sam Steele stood up. He faced the people in the room. "Now, everyone go home. Get back to your work and your lives. This investigation is over."

Then Sam Steele strode out of the room, followed by Chief Isadore and the freed young men.

12

Where is Fort Steele?

Sam Steele stood outside the courtroom and shook hands with the Chief and each of his men.

Matt and Emily shook hands with everyone, too.

"Thank you for bringing those blankets," Matt told the men. "I would have broken my arm, or worse, if I hadn't landed on them."

"You certainly made a grand entrance," said Sam Steele, laughing. "But all's well that ends well. Now, I must go. This has been a long,

eventful morning, and I'm ready for lunch. A big bowl of soup would be perfect."

"Soup!" said Emily. "That sounds delicious. I'd love some of my mom's chicken soup right now."

"Well, I hope you get some," said Steele. Then he unhitched his horse and, with a wave, galloped off.

The First Nations men and the chief waved to Emily and Matt and left too.

"I'm ready to go home and eat chicken soup," said Emily. "There's some soup left in the fridge. I can almost smell it."

"Let's see if the sled is ready to take us home," said Matt. "But first I have to report on everything that's happened. There's been no time before." Matt flipped on his recorder. "Ladies and Gentlemen. We met Sam Steele today and watched him investigate a murder. It was better than any movie."

Emily laughed. "I'm going to draw a picture of you falling into the courtroom," she said, as she pulled out her sketchbook and quickly drew a picture. "What do you think of this, Matt?"

Matt rolled his eyes. "I think I look silly," he said. "But falling inside the room did get us in to hear the investigation."

"You didn't fall in on purpose, did you?"

Matt smiled. "No way. I wouldn't risk cracking my head just for that. Come on, I'll race you."

Matt and Emily ran to the shack.

"It's a tie," said Emily pushing the door open.

"Phew! I don't think anyone's been here,"

said Matt peering around. "And yuck, I can still smell the skunk on our sled."

"We're also not alone."

"What do you mean?"

"Look what's all over those blankets!"

Mice scooted up and down.

"Yikes! How do we get them off?" said Matt.

"Shoo them off. Like this. Shoo. Shoo," said Emily, clapping her hands.

"Get lost," said Matt, stomping his feet.

But the mice wouldn't get off the blankets. They scurried up and down as if they were on a sidewalk.

"We have to do something else to get them off," said Emily.

"Like what?"

"Let's each grab one end of the blankets and yank."

"Okay. One. Two. Three. Yank!" said Matt.

They slid the blankets off the sled and the mice slid off, too.

"Look! The magic words are beginning to show up on the front of the sled. Hurry. Jump on," said Emily.

Matt and Emily hopped on.

They read the shimmery gold words.

You saw Sam Steele.
The men are free.
Now home is where
You want to be.

The sled began to move.

"Wait! There's a mouse sitting right behind me!" said Matt.

"Get him off," said Emily.

Matt grimaced. Then he picked the little creature up by its tail and placed it on the

ground. The startled rodent scampered away as the sled lifted up above the shack.

Soon they were sailing above the dusty streets of Galbraith's Ferry and up into the fluffy white cloud.

Back in Emily's tower room, the friends hopped off the sled.

"Yahoo! The smell is gone!" said Emily.

"Good old magic," said Matt, patting the sled.

"There's just one thing I still don't get. Why did the label on the Mountie's button say we were going to Fort Steele, but there was no Fort Steele?"

"Let's check it out on the Internet."

"Great idea!"

"Do you want to do that before or after chicken soup?" asked Matt.

"Before. I'm more curious than I am hungry!"

Emily and Matt ran down to the den and looked up Fort Steele and Galbraith's Ferry.

Emily read aloud from the screen:

Fort Steele
Fort Steele was originally a small settlement called Galbraith's Ferry, which was established in 1864. In 1888 the settlement's name was changed to Fort Steele to honour Superintendent Samuel Steele of the North-West Mounted Police, who peacefully settled a dispute between settlers and the Ktunaxa people.

"So that's the answer," said Emily. "It was named Fort Steele the year we were there, but not until after we left. And the two young boys we helped? They must have been members of the Ktunaxa Nation."

"I wonder if Sam Steele remembered that we had called it Fort Steele before it was actually named after him," said Matt.

"And I wonder what he thought about us knowing before anyone else. And why he didn't recognize us when we met him later in the Yukon?"

"Maybe it's 'cause we weren't in Galbraith's Ferry for very long, and years passed in his life before we saw him again. We'll probably never really know," said Matt.

Emily sighed. "Probably not. But Sam Steele was terrific. Let's toast him over a bowl of chicken soup. And then I'll sing a song about our adventure."

Matt groaned. "Please, don't."

"I won't," said Emily. "At least, not today."

MORE ABOUT...

After their adventure, Matt and Emily wanted to know more about the North-West Mounted Police and their role in calming tensions between settlers and First Nations. Turn the page for their favourite facts.

Emily's Top Ten Facts

1. Fort Steele is in the East Kootenay area of British Columbia, near the Rocky Mountains.

2. Galbraith's Ferry was named after John Galbraith, who started a ferry service on the Kootenay River.

3. John Galbraith made a fortune with his ferry. He charged passengers five dollars to cross and one dollar for each horse or mule. Later he opened a general store and bought a ranch.

4. In 1863, gold was discovered nearby in Wild Horse Creek. In less than one year, 5,000 fortune hunters had appeared. They found about 20 million dollars worth of gold dust and nuggets. A few years later, there was little gold left to find.

British Columbia was so busy with gold rushes in the late 1800s.
—M.

5. The town of Fisherville sprang up near Wild Horse Creek. It was destroyed about a year later when gold was discovered under the town.

Easy come, easy go! Goodbye, Fisherville! —M.

6. For the first ten years after Galbraith's Ferry was renamed Fort Steele, the town was a busy place. It was even called the capital of East Kootenay.

7. Miners also found coal, lead, and silver in the area around Fort Steele.

8. Then, in 1898, the British Columbia Southern Railway ran its tracks through Cranbrook instead of Fort Steele. Few people came to Fort Steele after that.

9. You can visit the Fort Steele Heritage Museum today and ride a wagon, take a tour by train, watch a show, and learn how to pan for gold.

10. When a movie called *North West Mounted Police* was shot in Hollywood in 1940, three hundred pine trees were brought in to make it look like the Canadian woods.

Matt's Top Ten Facts

1. The Ktunaxa people have lived in the Kootenay region for hundreds of generations, long before settlers showed up.

2. The Ktunaxa First Nations people became angry when settlers built ranches and fenced in the land.

3. Sam Steele was sent in to settle this dispute.

4. This is what a North-West Mounted Police officer did all day: patrolled; marched in drills; cleaned horse harnesses, stoves, and lanterns; cut firewood; and wind-proofed log houses.

5. Here's what a Mountie usually wore: a navy and gold pillbox hat, a red jacket, a brown belt, white gloves, navy pants with a gold stripe, and high black boots.

Just like in the movies!
-E.

6. The North—West Mounted Police (NWMP) was established in 1873. Sam Steele was the third person sworn in to the NWMP. He joined on Nov. 3, 1873, and signed on for three years.

7. Right before he left Fort Steele, the townspeople held a big sports day and riding exhibition.

8. There were lots of movies made about the Mounties in the 1930s and 1940s, but almost none of them were as famous as *Rose Marie.*

And luckily, in most of them the Mounties didn't sing!
—E.

9. In 1934, the Mounties started using dogs to help them with their work.

10. In 2001, there were about 1,200 registered members of the Ktunaxa Nation living in Canada. About 50% of those people were under 25.

So You Want to Know...

FROM AUTHOR FRIEDA WISHINSKY

When I was writing this book, my friends wanted to know more about the North-West Mounted Police and how important they were to Canada. I told them that the murder investigation in the book really took place and that Sam Steele, Chief Isadore, and the two accused First Nations men were involved. All the other characters in *On the Case* were made up. Here are other questions about the NWMP I answered:

When was the North-West Mounted Police created and by whom?

In 1873, the first prime minister of Canada, Sir John A. Macdonald, and the Canadian government formed the North-West Mounted Police.

Why did they create this police force?

The force was created to keep the peace in a large area of wilderness that stretched from the western border of Manitoba to the Rockies and up to the northernmost parts of Canada. It was also supposed to stop traders from the United States from selling alcohol to First Nations people in exchange for buffalo hides.

What was their first assignment?

In July 1874, a group of 275 Mounties set off near Winnipeg to trek across western Canada. With few supplies, they crossed through insect-infested land without access to much water and no real roads or bridges. When they finally reached their destination, their horses were exhausted, they were almost out of supplies, and many men were sick.

The Commissioner, George French, decided to divide the group in two. The weakest men took a longer but easier route toward Edmonton, and the stronger men took a shorter but tougher route towards the foothills of the Rockies.

When the journey was completed, the North-West Mounted Police were established on the western frontier to help keep the peace.

How did the Mounties stop the whisky traders?

In 1874, whisky traders from Montana had established a fort near what is now Lethbridge, Alberta. They called it Fort Whoop-Up, and they traded hides with the First Nations people in exchange for guns and whisky. The traders at the fort were well armed and even had a cannon. But when they heard the Mounties were coming, they left the fort and the Mounties took it without firing a shot. That event helped establish the reputation of the Mounties.

What else have the Mounties done over the years?

During the construction of the railroad across Canada, the Mounties helped deliver mail, keep records of births and deaths, and give farmers advice.

In 1885, they helped put down the North-West Rebellion and supervise the many people flocking out west.

During the Yukon Gold Rush of 1898, they maintained order and kept people safe from the dangerous conditions on the trails to the gold fields.

Less than 100 years later, they were involved in peacekeeping missions around the world, keeping others safe in Haiti, Namibia, and the former Yugoslavia.

When did they begin to be called the Royal Canadian Mounted Police?

In 1904, King Edward VII of England gave the North-West Mounted Police the title of "royal." In 1920, they called themselves by the name we use today: the Royal Canadian Mounted Police, or RCMP.

Coming next in the
Canadian Flyer Adventures Series...

Canadian Flyer Adventures
#13

Stop That Stagecoach!

Matt and Emily travel through the wilderness
of nineteenth-century Ontario.

For a sneak peek at the latest book in the series, visit:
www.owlkids.com
and click on the red maple leaf!

The *Canadian Flyer Adventures* Series

#1 Beware, Pirates!

#2 Danger, Dinosaurs!

#3 Crazy for Gold

#4 Yikes, Vikings!

#5 Flying High!

#6 Pioneer Kids

#7 Hurry, Freedom

#8 A Whale Tale

#9 All Aboard!

#10 Lost in the Snow

#11 Far from Home

#12 On the Case

Upcoming Book

Look out for the next book that will take
Emily and Matt on a new adventure:

#13 Stop That Stagecoach!

And more to come!

More Praise for the Series

"[Emily and Matt] learn more than they ever could have from a history textbook. Every book in this new series promises to shed light on a different chapter of Canadian history."
~ *MONTREAL GAZETTE*

"Readers are in for a great adventure."
~ *EDMONTON'S CHILD*

"This series makes Canadian history fun, exciting and accessible."
~ *CHRONICLE HERALD (HALIFAX)*

"[An] enthralling series for junior-school readers."
~ *HAMILTON SPECTATOR*

"...highly entertaining, very educational but not too challenging. A terrific new series."
~ *RESOURCE LINKS*

"This wonderful new Canadian historical adventure series combines magic and history to whisk young readers away on adventure...A fun way to learn about Canada's past."
~ *BC PARENT*

"Highly recommended."
~ *CM: CANADIAN REVIEW OF MATERIALS*

Teacher Resource Guides now available online. Please visit our website at
www.owlkids.com
and click on the red maple leaf to download tips and ideas for using the series in the classroom.

About the Author

Frieda Wishinsky, a former teacher, is an award-winning picture- and chapter-book author, who has written many beloved and bestselling books for children. Frieda enjoys using humour and history in her work, while exploring new ways to tell a story. Her books have earned much critical praise, including a nomination for a Governor General's Award in 1999. In addition to the books in the *Canadian Flyer Adventures* series, Frieda has published *What's the Matter with Albert?*, *A Quest in Time*, and *Manya's Dream* with Maple Tree Press. Frieda lives in Toronto.

About the Illustrator

Jean-Paul Eid has been drawing for as long as he can
remember. From a very young age he dreamed of becoming
a comic book artist, and liked to doodle cartoon characters
of his teachers in the margins of his school workbooks. At
the age of 20, he published his first comic in a magazine.
Since then, he has published four award-winning graphic
novels as well as several books for children. He has also
done illustrations for museums, children's magazines, and
film productions. Jean-Paul lives in Montreal, Quebec,
with his two children, Mathilde and Axel.

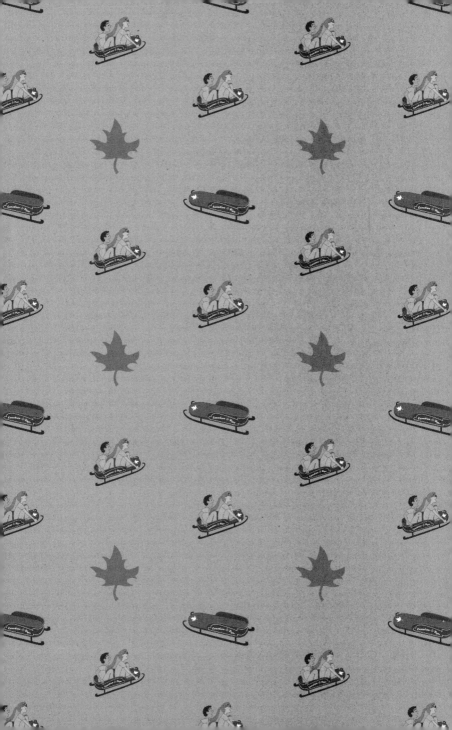